Mr Gum

in 'The Hound of Lamonic Bibber'

MINI BUMPER BOOK!

Shabba me whiskers! Andy Stanton's *Mr Gum* is winner of the Roald Dahl Funny Prize, the Red House Children's Book Award AND the Blue Peter Book Award for The Most Fun Story With Pictures. AND he's been shortlisted for LOADS of other prizes too! It's barking bonkers!

PRAISE FOR *Mr Gum*:

'Do not even think about buying another book – This is gut-spillingly funny.' Alex, aged 13

'It's hilarious, it's brilliant . . . Stanton's the Guv'nor, The Boss.' Danny Baker, BBC London Radio

'Funniest book I have ever and will ever read . . . When I read this to my mum she burst out laughing and nearly wet herself . . . When I had finished the book I wanted to read it all over again it was so good.' Bryony, aged 8

'Funny? You bet.' Guardian

'Andy Stanton accumulates silliness and jokes in an irresistible, laughter-inducing romp.' Sunday Times

'Raucous, revoltingly rambunctious and nose-snortingly funny.' Daily Mail

'David Tazzyman's illustrations match the irreverent sparks of word wizardry with slapdash delight.' Junior Education

'This is weird, wacky and one in a million.' Primary Times

'It provoked long and painful belly laughs from my daughter, who is eight.' Daily Telegraph

'As always, Stanton has a ball with dialogue, detail and devilish plot twists.' Scotsman

'We laughed so much it hurt.' Sophie, aged 9

'You will laugh so much you'll ache in places you didn't know you had.' First News

'A riotous read.' Sunday Express

'It's utterly bonkers and then a bit more - you'll love every madcap moment.' TBK Magazine

'Chaotically crazy.' Jewish Chronicle

'Designed to tickle young funny bones.' Glasgow Herald

'A complete joy to read whatever your age.'
This is Kids' Stuff

'The truth is a lemon meringue!' Friday O'Leary

'They are brilliant.' Zoe Ball, Radio 2

'Smooky palooki! This book is well brilliant.' Jeremy Strong

Judith, Dave, Max and Miranda for
Got to SOUL have!
Andy love

For loads of
Mr Gum fun check out
www.egmont.co.uk/mrgum

Also by Andy Stanton:

You're a Bad Man, Mr Gum!
Mr Gum and the Biscuit Billionaire
Mr Gum and the Goblins
Mr Gum and the Power Crystals
Mr Gum and the Dancing Bear
What's for Dinner, Mr Gum?
Mr Gum and the Cherry Tree
Mr Gum and the Secret Hideout

EGMONT
We bring stories to life

First published 2009 and in full extended version 2011 by Egmont UK Limited, 239 Kensington High Street London W8 6SA

Text copyright © 2009 and 2011 Andy Stanton
Illustration copyright © 2009 and 2011 David Tazzyman

The moral rights of the author and illustrator have been asserted

ISBN 978 1 4052 6188 3

1 3 5 7 9 10 8 6 4 2

A CIP catalogue record for this title is available from the British Library

Printed and bound in Italy

Mr Gum
in 'The Hound of Lamonic Bibber'
MINI BUMPER BOOK!

Andy Stanton

Illustrated by
David Tazzyman

Contents

Some of the crazy old townsfolk from Lamonic Bibber

Mrs Lovely

Friday O'Leary

Billy William
the Third

Old Granny

Mr Gum

Martin
Launderette

Alan Taylor

Polly

Introduction

It had been a fine dinner, a fine dinner indeed. Roast beef with potatoes and horseradish sauce, followed by the biggest, most delicious **Plum Ruffian** you've ever laid eyes on. But now Friday O'Leary sat back, burped once and addressed his guests.

'Enough of all this sitting around shovelling food down our throats like vulgar beasts and laying eyes on **Plum Ruffians**,' said he. 'Let us retire to the study, where I will startle your imaginations with one of the most incredible stories ever told.'

So nine-year-old Polly and little Alan Taylor, the gingerbread headmaster who was no taller than a common pencil, followed Friday into his study. And there they sat in deep leather armchairs, marvelling at their friend's collection of interesting items from around the world: rare talking flowers, a missing piece of the Bayeux tapestry which showed all the soldiers disco dancing, a tiny pony who lived in a milk bottle, a book written by a flea – and many more things besides.

'What're these things doin' here, Frides?' said Polly, pointing to a great pair of rusted old bells which hung above the fireplace.

'They are the legendary Bells of Charlie Nest,' said Friday. 'They once belonged to a fearsome American baker called Charlie Nest. And here's a curious thing: they still ring out whenever someone buys a bread roll anywhere on earth.'

'And what about that?' said Alan Taylor, pointing to a large bronze head that stood in the corner of the room looking proud and fierce. 'Where's that from?'

'I've no idea,' said Friday. 'It just walked in here one afternoon and I can't get rid of it. Sometimes if you look in its mouth it's filled with sweets. But other times it's just insects or cotton wool. Which is why I call it "Gigantic Mr Unpredictableface".'

Outside, the snow was falling, soft and stealthy like strange frozen music. The wind beat against the doors and windows of the secret cottage – let me in, let me in. But inside, all was well. The fire flickered in the grate, Gigantic Mr Unpredictableface stood silent and still and the cat purred contentedly on the hearth.

'I didn't know you had a cat,' said Alan Taylor, going over to stroke it.

'I haven't,' said Friday, and instantly the cat vanished.

'Now,' he continued, settling back in his chair and crossing his nose. 'It is time to tell you my story. For as you may know, I am not only a wonderful old fellow who cooks delicious roast beef and **Plum Ruffians**. I am also a mighty detective with the brains of an owl. In my time, I have solved many amazing mysteries including **The Mystery of the Oriental Crab, The Mystery of the Oriental Egg, The Mystery of the**

Oriental Necklace, and The Mystery of Why So Many Mysteries Are Just the Word "Oriental" followed by Some Random Object.

'But is it easy being a detective, you ask?' he continued. 'No, it is not! Oh, I have faced many dangers, including terrible poisons! Guns! Traps! Swords! And a man who kept creeping up on me and tapping me on one shoulder but when I turned around he was actually standing behind my other shoulder for a trick! It was terrifying!

'However, difficult and dangerous as these mysteries were, none of them can compare to my most incredible case of all – The Hound of Lamonic Bibber. I have never spoken about that case and I never will! I have vowed never to breathe a word about it to anyone. Never! I'm sorry, but my mind is made up. I absolutely refuse to talk about it.'

'Oh, go on,' said Alan Taylor.

'OK, then,' said Friday. 'The mystery begins many, many years ago, before either of you were born –'

'No, it don't,' said Polly. 'It was only a couple of years ago, remember? In facts, I helped you solve it.'

'Oh, yes,' said Friday. 'OK. The mystery begins not quite so many years ago after all. It was a night just like this one – snowy as a whipper, it was! Oh, the snow was falling like –'

'It wasn't snowin', Frides,' said Polly. 'It was foggy.'

'Oh, yes,' said Friday. 'That's right.'

'You really are an idiot,' said a tulip from a vase on the mantelpiece. 'Tell the story properly.'

'Sorry, rare talking flower,' said Friday. And, lowering his voice by getting out of his chair and lying face-down on the carpet, Friday started once more to tell his tale.

'The fog was creeping in,' said he. 'Creeping along over the wild and wiley moors. And as it crept it swayed and it swirled.

'Swirl,' whispered Friday in the flickering firelight. 'Swirl. Swirl. Swirl . . .'

Chapter 1

Terror in the Fog

Swirl, swirl, swirl.

The fog snaked its way through the midnight streets of Lamonic Bibber, thick and cold, and silent as an assassin.

Swirl, swirl, swirl.

The fog crept up to Boaster's Hill and pounced

all over it like a sinister dentist.

Swirl.

The fog did a bit more swirling.

No swirl.

The fog forgot to swirl and just hung around doing nothing.

Swirl, swirl, swirl.

Then it remembered, and went about its business once more. The fog gripped the town in its cold clammy fingers and even the moon was too scared to come out and fight it.

On the high street a single light was shining through the fog. It was coming from the butcher's shop, Billy William the Third's Right Royal Meats. And if you listened carefully, you could just make out the voices coming from within.

'Right, I got a brilliant move,' growled the first voice. 'I'm gonna move me Bishop over there an' smash your Queen up right in her stupid face!'

'Oh, yeah?' rasped the second voice. 'Well, I'm gonna fart all over your Bishop with this one what looks like a little horse!'

And if you had risked a glance through the greasy window you would have seen the owners of those voices, bathed in the flickering light of a candle made from mutton fat. For hunched over the counter were Billy William the butcher, and his filthy pal, Mr Gum. Yes, Mr Gum, with his scraggy red beard and his bloodshot eyes that stared out at you like an octopus curled up in a bad cave. The hideous pair were deep in thought, playing a game of chess as if their stinking lives depended upon it.

But wait! Outside the butcher's shop, something was stirring in the fog. Something large. Something that padded along on all fours. Something that was about to accidentally walk really hard into a lamppost –

GRRFF!

The muffled sound of an animal in pain rang out, but Mr Gum and Billy were so deep in concentration that they didn't even look up at the noise.

Outside in the darkness, the thing dusted itself off. It padded through the fog some more. Then it threw back its big shaggy head, and suddenly the night was filled with a blood-curdling

HA-ROOOOOOOOOOOOOWwwwWLLLL!

All over Lamonic Bibber the townsfolk trembled to hear that roar. And a little boy called Bradley did such a bad mess in his pyjamas that they had to be given to the charity shop the very next day.

HA-ROOOOOOOOOOOOOWWWWLLLL!

'Help! Look out!' cried little Bradley. 'There's a beast on the loose in Lamonic Bibber!'

And with that he ran downstairs, hopped into

his father's car and drove to South America, where he became a mighty priest. And in all his llong days ruling over the llamas of that lland, Bradley never once spoke of Lamonic Bibber and what he had glimpsed in the fog that night.

Chapter 2

The Next Morning

'NOOOOOOOOOOOOOO!'

The unhappy cry echoed through the early morning air, bringing people running from all over town. And there, still attached to the exclamation mark at the end of the 'NOOOOOOOOOOOOOO!' which was coming from her mouth, they found –

'Old Granny!' exclaimed Jonathan Ripples, the fattest man in town. 'What is it?'

But Old Granny hardly noticed Jonathan Ripples, even though he was about the size of a small circus tent. She was gazing with horror at her garden. Her ancient rose bushes from before the War had been trampled into the mud. And her secret supply of sherry had been emptied into the ornamental bird bath.

'Who did this?' Old Granny asked the starlings

who were playing in the bath – but they were far
too drunk to tell her. One of them had a little
party hat on.

And the destruction didn't stop there. All over town, gardens had been ruined. Small trees had been uprooted, dustbins had been overturned and a garden gnome called **Fishin' Tony** had died of a heart attack. It was horrible.

'My lawn is torn and now I'm forlorn!' wailed Beany McLeany, who loved things that rhymed.

'My shiny new bike!' sobbed a little girl called Peter. 'I left it outdoors and now look – it's been smashed into six pieces! No, hold on – eight pieces!

No, hold on – fourteen!'

'My expensive hedge!' wept David Casserole, the town mayor. 'Nothing's happened to it at all! But imagine if it had, that would have been awful!'

'No, hold on – twenty-three pieces!' sobbed the little girl called Peter.

Yes, the whole town of Lamonic Bibber was in a terrible state. It seemed that everyone had a sad tale to tell, from the tiny baby whose pram had been covered in spit, to the dozens of tramps who'd been pushed into the duck pond while they slept peacefully in the gutter.

But after all the crying had been cried and the last teardrop had been teardropped – that's when the questions began:

'Who could have wreaked such terrible havoc and destruction?'

'Who would even dream of doing such a thing to our little town?'

'Is "teardropped" even a real word?'

At last one man stepped forward with the answers. It was Martin Launderette, who ran the launderette.

'Firstly, I saw who did this thing to our town,' he said. 'Secondly, "teardropped" isn't a real word at all. And thirdly, it was no human who did this deed. It was a hound. And not just any hound – but a gigantic great tangler of a bark-monster. I saw him last night with my very own eyes that I've known and trusted for years.'

'Martin, just how big was this dog that you supposedly saw?' asked Jonathan Ripples.

'About as big,' whispered Martin dramatically, 'about as big as that dog over there.' And he pointed across the street to where a massive whopper of a dog played happily with an old chip packet, his long golden fur waving merrily in the breeze.

'Now hang on, Mr Laund'rettes,' said a little girl called Polly, who is one of the heroes of this story even though she's only nine. 'Jake's the friendliest, happiest woofdog what ever done bounced through the streets of this town! You better not be accusin' him of all this!'

'I'm not accusing anyone,' muttered Martin Launderette. 'I'm just saying Jake's ruined people's gardens before, that's all. And anyway, who do you think left *this* everywhere?'

He pointed to the clumps of golden fur that lay scattered on the ground. The pieces of little Peter's bicycle were covered with the stuff.

'That fur could be there for a million innocent reasons,' replied Polly indignantly. 'For instances, maybe it fell off a fur tree. An' you oughtn'ts to go whippin' up hatreds towards big friendly dogs without no proofs!'

'Well, there was *something* out there last night,' said Martin Launderette, his eyes darting madly from face to face in the crowd. 'What if it comes back?'

'It's true,' quaked Old Granny, who had been lapping sherry from her bird bath all the while.

'It's true,' shivered the tramps in the duck pond. 'What if it comes back?'

'Well, now,' said Jonathan Ripples, stepping forward boldly, his chins vibrating in the breeze.

'If it comes back it shall have me to contend with. Because yes! I shall guard the town tonight. And if there IS a hound out there, I'll sit on him until he's nothing but a dog-flavoured pancake!'

Chapter 3

Back at the
Butcher's Shop

'Look at 'em all,' laughed Mr Gum, as he watched the crowd from Billy William the Third's Right Royal Meats.

'Jumpin' to conclusions like that! What a bunch of ignorant grapes!'

'Ha ha ha,' laughed Billy William, mopping up some pig's blood from the floor with his tongue. 'Ha ha ha.'

'Ha ha ha,' laughed Mr Gum.

'Ho ho ho,' laughed Billy. 'It's funty!'

'Yeah,' agreed Mr Gum. 'It's very "funty" indeed.'

'Another "game of chess" tonight then?' suggested Billy.

'That's right, Billy me boy,' nodded Mr Gum, sucking a lump of rotten pâté from his scruffy red beard. 'Another "game of chess" it is. Ha ha ha ha ha!'

.

Chapter 4

A Bit More Terror in the Fog

Swirl. Swirl. Swirl.

That night the fog returned. It didn't even bother to phone ahead and check it was OK to come over. It just strolled into town as it pleased, flapping all over the place like an unwelcome ostrich on a train.

Once again, most of the shops on the high street stood dark and silent. Once again, a single light was shining in the butcher's shop. And once again, I'm about to say 'once again'. Because once again, anyone glancing through the greasy window could have seen 'em – those two filthmongers, Mr Gum and Billy William, hunched over the counter at their chessboard.

'Right, I got a brilliant move,' growled Mr Gum. 'I'm gonna move me Bishop over there an' smash your Queen up right in her stupid face!'

'Oh, yeah?' rasped Billy. 'Well, I'm gonna fart all over your Bishop with this one what looks like a little horse!'

♟ ♟ ♟

'What on earth am I doing out here?' trembled Jonathan Ripples as he patrolled the dark streets with only a broken torch and a double cheeseburger for company. He wished he hadn't volunteered to guard the town. What a stupid idea that had been!

He held up the cheeseburger, flapping it open and shut in his chubby hand like a puppet.

'Don't worry,' said Jonathan Ripples in a funny little voice, as if it were the cheeseburger talking.

'Everything's going to be aaaaaall-right.'

'Oh, Burger Boy!' said Jonathan Ripples gratefully. 'Do you really think so?'

'Yes,' squeaked Burger Boy. 'Everything's going to be just –'

HA-ROOOOOOOOOOOOWwwwwLLLLL!

The savage noise cut through the night air like an aeroplane made of teeth.

'Uh-oh,' said Burger Boy.

HA-ROoooOoooOOoooOoWwwwwLLLLL!

'I think it's the Hound,' said Burger Boy. 'Try and stay calm –'

'THE HOUND!' yelped Jonathan Ripples, taking off down the road, Burger Boy clutched tightly in his hand. He tried to run but everything had turned to slow motion, like in a scary film or when your mum goes shopping and drags you round about ten million different shops trying to save twenty pence on a new kettle.

HA-ROOOOOOOOOOOOOWWWWLLLL!

'THE HOOOOOUUUND!' screamed Jonathan Ripples – but then he tripped and hit his head hard against the cobblestones. And he was out like a fat light.

Chapter 5

The Townsfolk Point Their Townsfingers

*I*t was Martin Launderette who discovered Jonathan Ripples lying in the road the next morning, covered in fur, dribble and cheeseburger crumbs.

'Martin?' groaned Jonathan Ripples, holding his aching head. 'What happened? And why are there three of you? And where's Burger Boy?'

'I'll tell you what happened!' snorted Martin Launderette, as a crowd gathered to see what was going on. 'The Hound came back, that's what happened! And there he is now!' he yelled, pointing to where Jake the dog was frolicking happily with a sparrow not twenty yards away. 'HE's the one that's been terrorising Lamonic Bibber! Jake, I mean, not the sparrow,' he added.

The townsfolk looked from the fur on
Jonathan Ripples' jumper to the fur on Jake's
back. They looked from the dribble on Jonathan
Ripples' leg to the drool slurping out of
Jake's mouth. Could it be true? Could
Jake be behind the whole thing?

'Look at his eyes,' whispered
Old Granny, taking a sip of sherry
to calm her nerves. 'They're the
eyes of an animal!'

'Sometimes good dogs turn naughty,' whispered the little girl called Peter. 'It's true, I saw a documentary about it called *Mummy, Why Did Rover Eat Grandpa?*'

'Is Jake really the dog in the fog and the smog?' whispered Beany McLeany.

'Of course he is!' spat Martin Launderette. 'It's obvious!'

'No, it isn't!' cried Polly. 'It isn't obvious even

slightly at all! Has you all got "**OUT OF ORDER**" signs on your brains?'

But no one paid Polly any heed.

'Jake the dog is a criminal!' shouted Martin Launderette. 'First he attacks our gardens, then he attacks Jonathan Ripples in the fog and murders Burger Boy – where will it all end? We have to get rid of him! Let's send him to Australia on the next boat!'

'Martin Launderette is right!' cried Old Granny,

drunkenly waving her bottle of sherry.

'Australia's where he belongs, with all those other naughty dogs!' shouted the little girl called Peter – and soon they were all at it, shouting at poor Jake and poking their tongues out at him and trying to make daddy-long-legses go near him to frighten him.

'What in the name of marmalade's happened to you lot?' cried Polly. 'Sure as squirrels is squirrels, I gots to do somethin' 'bout this!'

Chapter 6

The Greatest Detective of Them All

*L*ater that morning, a wonderful old fellow called Friday O'Leary was sitting alone in his secret cottage in the woods. He was watching a film on TV about a man sitting alone in a secret cottage in the woods who was watching a film on TV about a man sitting alone in a secret cottage in the woods who was watching a film on TV about a man sitting alone in a secret cottage in the woods who was watching a –

Suddenly – KNOCK! KNOCK! – the doorbell rang.

'Thank goodness,' said Friday, jumping up from his armchair. 'That film was starting to drive me crazy.'

He threw open the door and there was Polly, standing on the doorstep with a look in her eye

that meant business and a hairclip in her hair
that meant she'd recently bought a new hairclip.

'Polly!' smiled Friday. 'What
brings you all the way out
here, little miss?'

'Oh, Frides,' sighed
Polly, 'I hardly knows
how to begin.'

'Begin at the beginning,'
said Friday wisely,
tapping his nose.

'And when you get to a bit you can't remember, just make it up. That's what I do.'

△ △ △

So Polly told Friday all about it. How the townsfolk were blaming Jake for the night-time attacks, even though they had no proof – and how they were going to send him off to Australia for the crime.

'So who's really behind it, if it's not Jake?' said Friday when Polly had finished. 'It's a mystery. But luckily you've come to the right place. When it comes to solving amazing mysteries, I am the greatest detective of them all.'

'Are you sure?' said Polly.

'Oh, yes,' said Friday, twirling his imaginary detective's moustache grandly. 'Just listen to this and you'll know it must be a fact!'

And slipping on a pair of tap-dancing shoes, he burst into flame. I mean, he burst into song:

I'M A DETECTIVE

You know I'm not a florist or
a cowboy on the farm
I'm not a lizard keeper at the zoo
I am no baby with a dummy
Always crying for his mummy
So if you ever ask me what I do . . .

CHORUS:

I'm a detective!
I find the clues!
I find the things that others overlook
And I write them down in my little black book
And then I say 'I've solved the crime'
And everyone says 'hooray!'

It's true I'm not a preacher or a teacher
Or a smeacher
You'll never find me cleaning out the drains
I don't work at a factory
That would not be satisfactory
Instead, I use my cunning and
my brains . . .

CHORUS:

I'm a detective!
I've got a hat!
The clues that criminals drop
I tend to spot
And I think about things an awful lot
And then I say, 'I've solved the crime!'
And everyone says 'hooray!'
Yes, everyone says 'hooray!'

Yes, everyone says, 'hooray for Friday!
He's the funkiest, unbelievab'list
Most spectacular, chasing bad
guys-est, Sherlock Holmes-iest,
clue-discov'ring-est
Detective bloke we've ever, EVER
seeeeeeeen!'

'Well, now do you believe me?' panted Friday.

'I thinks so,' said Polly.

'THE TRUTH IS A LEMON MERINGUE!' yelled Friday, as he sometimes liked to do. 'Let's get detecting!'

Chapter 7

A Clue or Two

Back at Billy William's butcher's shop, Mr Gum and Billy were having a deep and meaningful discussion about life.

'I'll tell you who I hate,' said Mr Gum thoughtfully, as he chewed on an out-of-date pork chop, 'everyone in the world, includin' meself.'

'An' I'll tell you what annoys me,' said Billy,

snorting a bunch of entrails up his nose, 'absolutely everythin'.'

'An' I'll tell you what I can't stand,' said Mr Gum. 'Runnin' out of beer. Go an' steal us a few more cans, Billy, me old candlestick.'

'Righty-o,' said Billy.

'An' be quick,' Mr Gum shouted after him. 'I ain't got all day. Shabba me whiskers!' he muttered. 'It's hard work bein' me. I'd better have a nap.'

And he lay down on the filthy counter, shut his

eyes and fell into a half-drunken doze.

§ § §

RAP! RAP! RAP!

'Eh?' said Mr Gum, starting awake. 'What's that?'

'We knows you're in there, Mr Gum!' yelled a voice. 'Let us in!'

Muttering to himself, Mr Gum unlocked the door. 'Jibbers!' he scowled when he saw Polly and Friday O'Leary standing there on the pavement.

'What do you two meddlers want?'

'Mr Gum, we want to ask you some questions,' said Friday. 'Questions about the mysterious Hound that's been hounding this town like some sort of hound.'

'Why would I know anythin' about that?' growled Mr Gum, scratching furiously at his dirty red beard.

'Cos you are the worst, Mr Gum,' said Polly. 'Whenever bad stuff happens 'round here you're usually behinds it, or at least standin' quite nears it.

'Now, tell us what you been up to last night when that Hound-dog done attacked Mr Ripples – an' don't you do no lies on me, you rascal de la splarscal!'

'Why,' said Mr Gum, 'I been stayin' 'round here at Billy's. We been playin' chess, that's all. See?' And he pointed to a grimy chessboard which sat on the shop counter.

'Hmm,' said Friday. 'Mind if we take a look?'

'Do what you like, you weirdoes,' scowled

Mr Gum. 'See if I care.'

Friday and Polly stepped nervously through the door. It was horrible in there. Bones and bits of meat littered the floor. The walls were crawling with mould. And everywhere you looked there were flies, buzzing through the air or feasting on the slop buckets Billy left out for them. Billy William loved those flies and he knew all their names, even the babies. They were like a family to him.

'Where is Billy, anyway?' asked Friday, brushing a bluebottle called Gary from his hair.

'Billy had to nip out to stea– I mean, to buy some beer,' growled Mr Gum, 'not that it's any of your business, Captain Nosey.'

'Well, who's that then?' said Polly, pointing to a figure lying sprawled on the floor. 'It looks like Billy to me.'

'Borklers!' Mr Gum swore under his breath. 'Oh, yeah, there he is. He must've come back while I was asleep.'

Friday nudged Billy's arm with the toe of his boot. 'Is he all right? He's not moving.'

'He's FINE,' snapped Mr Gum. 'He prob'ly just had too much to drink. Now, forget about Billy, you wanna see this chessboard or not?'

Polly ran her finger over the wooden chessboard and shuddered. The thing was slippery with grease and entrails.

'See?' said Mr Gum triumphantly. 'Me an' Billy

loves our chess. An' if that's a crime then I dunno what this town's comin' to.'

$$♟ ♟ ♟$$

'Well, they're def'nitely up to somethin',' exclaimed Polly when they were back outside. 'Did you notice how nervous Mr Gum looked when we was doin' our 'mazin' detectiver stuff?'

'Oh, yes,' lied Friday, 'definitely.'

'An' look,' said Polly, holding up her finger. It

was covered with grease from the chessboard. But there was something else there too.

'Fur,' said Friday, screwing his eyes up like he'd once seen a cool detective do on TV. 'Just like the fur when the Hound attacked.'

'Them two's up to somethin',' said Polly. 'But what we gonna do 'bout it, Frides?'

Friday thought for a moment. Then he thought for another moment. Then he thought for an hour and a half. 'We're going to drink coffee,' he said finally. 'Lots and lots of coffee. Except for you, Polly, you're only nine. You can just look at a photo of some coffee instead.'

'But why, Frides, why?'

'Simple, little miss,' replied Friday, twirling his imaginary detective's moustache so hard it nearly became real for a moment. 'We need to stay awake, because tonight we're going on a stake-out. Plus I quite fancy a coffee anyway.'

Chapter 8

The Stake-out

Swirl.

Night time once again and the fog was back, thick and whirling. Almost everyone in town was fast asleep in bed. Not the same bed, that would be weird. Different beds. In the zoo, all the animals had been switched off for the night. A copy of that morning's **Lamonical Chronicle** blew along the deserted pavement, its headline plain to see:

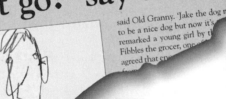

amonic Bibber's Second Best, & Only, Newspaper

The Lamonical Chronicle

'Jake the dog must go!' say towns

» 'I'll kick him out if it's the first thing I do!' vows Martin Launderette

» 'Then I'll kick him out again, just to make sure,' he adds

Manzilla Uprooster reports

For centuries, Lamonic Bibber has been famous for three things: having a stupid name, being haunted by the ghost of William Shakespeare, and being the only place in England where it is still le_ marry a bee. But now th_ remember ou_

said Old Granny. 'Jake the dog m_ to be a nice dog but now it's remarked a young girl by t Fibbles the grocer, one_ agreed that e_

'Stupid newspaper!' said Polly. She and Friday were crouched down behind a couple of dustbins on the high street, directly opposite the butcher's shop. That way they could lie in wait for the Hound and keep an eye on Mr Gum and Billy at the same time.

'Look,' whispered Polly as the night sky began to cloud over and a damp chill crept into the air, 'it's gonna be another right old fogger-me-smogger.'

'Good,' replied Friday, who had disguised

himself as an owl by drawing circles around his eyes and sticking a squeaky toy mouse in his mouth. 'That's exactly what we want. If it's foggy then the Hound will come out – if it really is a hound. And then we can catch it in our net – if it really is a net.'

'Are stake-outs always this borin'?' said Polly two hours later.

'**SQUEEK,**' replied Friday, chewing on the

toy mouse. 'It depends. Generally, in my experience –'

'Hold on,' whispered Polly. 'Somethin's happenin'.'

It was true. Up until that moment the butcher's shop had been completely dark. But now a candle had been lit, its flickering flame just visible through the thick fog.

'*SQUEEK*,' said Friday. 'Let's go and take a closer look.' Friday crept out from behind the dustbin and went slithering across the street on his stomach, keeping his eyes shut so he'd be invisible. Polly followed close behind.

And now they could see Mr Gum and Billy through the shop window. The two of them were hunched over the chessboard, Billy looking thoughtful with one hand to his chin, Mr Gum dangling his Bishop over the board, as if deciding exactly where to place it.

'Right, I got a brilliant move,' they heard Mr Gum growl. 'I'm gonna move me Bishop over there an' smash your Queen up right in her stupid face!'

'*SQUEEK*,' said Friday.

'They really are playing chess!'

'Yeah,' said Polly, 'but I reckons they're jus' fakin' it in case anyone's watchin' them. Any moment now they're gonna stop pretendin', sneak out the door an' go runnin' all over town destroyin' stuff up.'

'You mean –' began Friday.

'Yes,' whispered Polly, 'I reckons Martin Launderette only *thinks* he saw a Hound the other night. If you asks me, what he actually done saw was Mr Gum an' Billy disguised as –'

But at that moment a dreadful howl shattered the silence of the fog, a howl so terrifying that it would have reduced the most courageous eagle on earth to little more than a whimpering doughnut with a beak.

HA-ROOOOOOOOOOOOWWWWWLLLL!

'It's the Hound!' chuckled Friday.

'I mean – it's the Hound!' he screamed in terror.

'I don't understands,' said Polly, glancing back at the butcher's, where Mr Gum and Billy were still hunched over their game. 'I was so sure them two was behind it . . .'

HA-ROOOOOOOOOOOOWWWWLLLL!

'It seems you were mistaken, little miss,' said Friday. 'There really is a real Hound who's really on the loose for real! Now come on, Polly – after it!' he cried, taking off around the corner, his coat-tails flying out behind him. 'THE TRUTH IS A LEMON MERINGUE!'

'Frides! Frides!' Polly ran after her friend but it was no good – she was instantly lost in the swirling fog.

Swirl, swirl, swirl.

Polly ran up and down the damp cobblestones, the fog closing in all around her. Which way was which? What was what? She didn't have a clue what was going on. It was like being trapped inside a giant French exam.

HA-ROOOOOOOOOOOOOWWWWWLLLL!

HA-ROO
OOOOO
OOOOO
WWWWW
LLLL!

The sound seemed to come from right behind her.

HA-ROOOOOOOOOOOOOWWWWWLLLL!

Now it seemed to come from far away.

Was it to her left?

HA-
R
O
O
O
O
O
O
O
O
O
O
O
O
W
W
W
W
L
L
L
L
!

Or her right?

'SQUEEK. SQUEEK.'

'Frides, is that you?' shouted Polly.

What now? Was there a cow loose as well? It was impossible to tell what was happening. Visions of terrible snapping jaws filled Polly's mind, each tooth as sharp as those little spiky bits you get on pineapples . . . Eyes, red in the darkness, red – the colour of blood, the colour of danger, the colour of red things . . .

Polly felt something huge and heavy and furry land on her back.

A paw! she had time to think – and suddenly the fog wasn't just all around her, it seemed to actually be inside her mind, and the whole world went grey, and she was spinning, spinning towards the cobblestones . . .

Chapter 9

It Was All Just a Bad Dream

When Polly awoke she was back in her cosy pink bed, safe and sound.

'Oh, Mummy!' she exclaimed. 'What a terrible dream I just had! I was running through the fog and there was a horrid great doggie chasing me and –'

'There, there,' said Polly's mother kindly. 'It was only a bad dream. And today is your birthday, remember? Look what we've bought you.'

'*Oh, Mummy!*' exclaimed Polly, clapping her hands together. 'A new pony and an enormous castle made of chocolate!'

But unfortunately that wasn't the Polly in this story. That was a different Polly who lived in a mansion in New York City, miles and miles away from the little town of Lamonic Bibber.

'*La la la la la,*' sang the Polly who wasn't in

this story. 'I've never once been in danger in my whole life. I'm the luckiest little girl in the world!'

Chapter 10

It Wasn't All Just a Bad Dream

When the Polly in *this* story awoke it was still dark. She was lying outside in the cold and the fog, at the bottom of Boaster's Hill. And the Hound was right there with her, staring directly into her eyes.

'YOIFLE!' screamed Polly. And she fainted all over again.

🐇 🐇 🐇

It was some time later when Polly came to her senses. Through the thinning fog she could see the moon, gazing down upon her with its lonely silver smile, gazing down as if to offer comfort, gazing down as if to say, *Look out, Polly. Something's licking your knee.*

And it was true. A tongue, rough and wet, was

licking her knee. The Hound was licking her knee!

'YOIF–' she began. But then the fog cleared some more and she saw that it was none other than –

'Jake!' exclaimed Polly. 'But if you're out here in the middle of the night . . . I dunno what to think. Is it you what's the Hound after all? Say it isn't true, even though you can't do no words!'

HA-ROOOOOOOOOOOOOOWWWWLLLL!

The now familiar howl came again – but from the other side of town! It was followed by a distant cry –

'*SQUEEK. SQUEEK. SQUEEK.* THE TRUTH IS A LEMON MERINGUE!'

'So hang on,' said Polly slowly. 'Friday's still out there right now, chasin' the real Hound. An' that means you CAN'T be the Hound, Jakey! You're innocent! Oh, I knowed it!'

'BARK BARK BARK,' said Jake, licking Polly's eyebrows happily and making her laugh despite it all.

And Polly buried her face in the big dog's side and cried tears of relief and misery and happiness all rolled up into a brand new super-emotion called '*remippiness*'. And there she stayed, safe and warm until morning, stroking

Jake's soft golden fur and feeling him breathe in and out like the good dog he truly was.

Chapter 11

The Singing Detective

'What do we do now, Frides?' said Polly as they wandered the streets of the town, Jake at their side. 'We knows Jakey's innocent as a newborn baby peanut. But how we gonna proof it?'

Friday's imaginary moustache drooped sadly. He had been up all night chasing the Hound and he was cold and hungry and tired. And not only that, but his toy mouse had been eaten by a toy cat when he wasn't looking.

'Let's get some breakfast,' he said, 'that ought to cheer us up.'

But every café on the high street had the same sign in the window:

NO DOGS ALLOWED
APART FROM ONES THAT AREN'T JAKE

And every face they passed on the rainy streets

that morning told the same story of fear, resentment and not liking Jake very much.

'That dog's a menace,' trembled Old Granny, who had been drinking sherry all morning to calm her nerves. 'I'll be glad when he's gone!'

'Your big wet pet makes me very upset,' rhymed Beany McLeany.

'I don't like him either, even though I don't really know what's going on,' said a passing American tourist.

'Uh-oh,' said Polly as they approached the launderette, where a large crowd had gathered. 'This looks like troubles.'

And it was troubles. An enormous washing machine stood upon the pavement and standing on the washing machine, jiggling crazily up and down as it spun, was Martin Launderette.

'LOOK!' he yelled when he saw Jake approaching. 'There he is! He's not a dog! He's a devil in disguise! As a dog!'

'WOOF!' said Jake, rolling over on to his back, hoping for a friendly tickle.

'Have you ever seen such a terrifying beast?' spat Martin Launderette. 'But never fear, townsfolk. The boat to Australia leaves at nine o'clock tomorrow morning! And I'll personally ensure that dog's on it!'

'Hooray for Martin Launderette!' shouted the crowd. 'Hooray for Martin L!'

'Oh, Frides,' said Polly as they walked away, the cheers of the crowd still ringing in their ears. 'We gots one more night to proof Jake's innocences, or it's off to 'Stralia for him an' that's the last we'll ever see of his lovely paws. What we gonna do?'

'Um, I could sing "I'm A Detective" again,' suggested Friday.

'I don't supposes it will help much, Frides,' said Polly sadly. 'But go on, I knows how you loves your sing-songery.'

'OK,' said Friday, slipping into his tap-dancing shoes. 'Here goes!

I'M A DETECTIVE

You know I'm not a florist or a
cowboy on the farm
I'm not a lizard keeper at the zoo
I am no baby with a dummy
Always crying for his mummy
So if you ever –

– why, Polly, what on earth's the matter?'

But Polly barely heard him. She was frozen to the spot, her hand paused in mid-stroke through Jake's spongy tongue.

'What's wrong, little miss?' asked Friday again.

'I . . . It's . . . It's all . . . makin' senses,' whispered Polly. 'It's all comin' together.' Every single hair on her head was standing on end. Her arms were covered in goosebumps. Her geese were covered in armbumps. It felt like someone had poured special **Detective Sauce™** into her head and was cooking her brains in a *Microwave of Knowledge™*.

'Frides,' said Polly slowly, 'can you sing that last bit again?'

'I am no baby with a dummy, always crying for his mummy,' sang Friday – and that was it. The final piece of the puzzle slotted into place and Polly's brain went '**DING!**' so loudly even Friday heard it.

'HOFFLESTICKS!' she exclaimed. 'Now I knows

how them villains was able to get 'way with it, the sneakies! Come on, Frides,' said Polly. 'You're gonna need loads more coffee to keeps you awake. An' I'm a-gonna needs to look at a photo of the strongest cup of coffee what's ever been brewed. We gotta do another stake-out – an' we gotta do it tonights!'

Chapter 12

The Hound of Lamonic Bibber

Swirl.

The final night – and the fog had returned. Polly and Friday crouched outside the butcher's shop, hardly daring to breathe in case somebody heard them, but hardly daring not to breathe in case they died from not breathing. It was a difficult one.

Swirl. Swirl. Swirl.

Thicker than ever, the fog crept secretively through the town, wrapping itself around lampposts and dustbins like a ghost, turning everything it touched into a mystery.

''Tis the worst fog this town has ever seen,' whispered Old Granny. ''Tis the worst –'

'Go back home, Old Granny,' whispered Friday kindly. 'You're not meant to be in this bit of the story.'

'Sorry,' said Old Granny, who was a bit drunk.

And taking a sip of sherry from the bottle she always kept hidden in the fog she toddled off home, leaving Polly and Friday to get on with their stake-out.

It was all down to them now. If they'd guessed right, Jake's name would be cleared forever and he'd be welcomed back to run and romp and roll through the streets of the town like always.

But if they'd guessed wrong? Well, then. That was the end for old Jakey boy. He'd be carted off to Australia like a sack of wizards, and Polly would never see him again, except in her tears. Perhaps, she thought, other children would one day play with him and ride upon his back for their fun. Other children who were unaware that he'd once been called Jake. They'd probably name him 'Stuart' or 'Bouncyface' or 'Sydney Opera Dog'. It didn't bear thinking about.

'Not much longer now,' whispered Polly, her teeth chattering against the cold. And even as she spoke, a candle was lit inside the butcher's shop. Polly risked a glance through the window and saw the two men in their usual positions, hunched over their game of chess.

'OK,' said Friday. 'They're ready. Let's go.'

The detectives crept around the side of the butcher's shop and tiptoed up the fire escape.

Bodies flat against the tarmac roof, they peered down upon the stinking bins and rubbish that littered the alleyway below.

For a few minutes more they lay there in silence. It seemed like nothing was going to happen.

Swirl, swirl, swirl.

The fog enshrouded them, tugging at their sleeves, whispering like a dead man into their ears.

Then . . .

Creeeeaaaaaaak . . .

The back door to the shop creaked softly open.

Shuffle, shuffle, shuffle.

A large bulky shape padded out into the misty alleyway.

It was the beast that had terrorised the town for over ten chapters!

It was the monster that haunted everyone's darkest dreams!

It was the Hound of Lamonic Bibber!

HA-ROOOOOOOOOOOOOWWWWLLLL!

Even though Polly knew better, a shiver ran up her spine. What if she was wrong? What if she was messing with forces she didn't understand? The fog swirled all around, striking fear into her heart and fog into her nostrils, and for just one moment Polly was tempted to drive to South America, become a priest and forget about the whole thing.

'But no,' she whispered to herself through clenched teeth. 'I've come too far to give up like a

pathetic cornflake! Come on, Friday! RELEASE
THE NET!'

And that was the secret signal for Friday to
release the net.

HA-ROOO?

The Hound looked up.

The net came down.

The Hound's bloodshot eyes flashed furiously.

HA-ROOOOOOOOOOOOOWWWWWLLLL!

But it was no good howling at the net. The net wasn't scared. It was a net.

GRRR!! SNRURURHSH! MMMMMMMFFFFF!

The Hound staggered like a mad thing around the alleyway, overturning bins of rotten meat, clumps of fur flying everywhere.

But the more it tried to tear itself free, the more it clawed and pawed and roared, the more entangled it became. Until eventually it gave up and collapsed in a filthy heap, breathing in great ragged gasps, huge green flies buzzing all around it like dirty spaceships circling a horrible new planet called STENCHULOS 9.

Cautiously the detectives climbed down from the roof and approached their hideous catch.

'Look,' whispered Polly, training her torch-beam upon the humped-up shape. 'There can't be no doubt 'bout it. This is the naughty shambler what's been doin' all them bads.'

Yes, it was true. The Hound's hide was covered with stains and stinks from its night-time adventures. Its fur was streaked with grass and mud, it reeked of Old Granny's sherry – and the handlebars of little Peter's bicycle were still stuck to one of its legs.

'So there really was a Hound after all,' nodded Friday wisely. 'Just as I thought.'

'But wait, Frides.' Polly was down on her hands and knees in the filthy alleyway as she pulled away the heavy net. Screwing her face up with bravery and facial muscles, she dug both hands deep into the Hound's shaggy fur and flung it aside to reveal . . .

'**W**ell,' yawned Friday O'Leary, rising from his chair. 'That's more or less everything that happened. Goodnight, everyone. I'm going to bed.'

'What?!' protested Alan Taylor, his electric muscles sparking with indignation. 'You can't end the story there, that was the most exciting bit!'

'Yeah, come on,' said Polly. 'Finish the story, Frides. Else you'll make Alan Taylor cry, an' then his face'll go well soggy an' then we'll has to hang him up on the clothesline to dry out an' then cruel children will come along an' play a game where they throw melons at him to score points.'

'Very well,' replied Friday. 'I will continue the story if you can guess what I'm holding in my hand. You get three guesses.'

'Is it a penny?' asked Alan Taylor.

'Nope,' replied Friday.

'Is it a leaf?' asked Polly.

'Nope,' replied Friday, drawing the curtains against the snowy night outside. 'One more wrong guess and that's it. I'm off to bed.'

'Hmm,' said Alan Taylor. 'Is it a miniature 1:16 scale model of a very rare "Henrick & Son" five pedal orchestral upright grand piano in exquisite burl walnut, with beautifully carved legs, richly detailed mouldings and elegant rosewood panelled sides, originally called the "Style 34 Concert Grand" according to its original sales catalogues, and possessed of an unmatched tone, lending it a warmth and clarity which places it amongst the best in the world in terms of concert recitals?'

'Yes,' sighed Friday, opening his hand

to show them the tiny piano, which was being played by a talented little insect called Ludwig van Beetlehoven. 'Fair enough, you win. Now, where was I?'

'You were behind the butcher's shop, you idiot,' said the tulip from its vase on the mantelpiece. 'You were just about to find out what you'd caught in that stupid net of yours.'

'Ah, yes,' said Friday, settling back in his chair. 'Thank you, rare talking flower. So – Polly was down on her hands and knees in the filthy alleyway . . .'

Polly was down on her hands and knees in the filthy alleyway as she pulled away the heavy net. Screwing her face up with bravery and facial muscles, she dug both hands deep into the Hound's shaggy fur and flung it aside to reveal . . .

'Woof,' scowled Mr Gum, his bloodshot eyes blazing like lanterns.

'Woof, woof,' said Billy William, his arms wrapped tight around Mr Gum's waist. A tail made from rope hung limply from the back of his apron. 'Bark bark bark.'

'It's no good tryin' to fool us no more, you bad

men,' said Polly. 'We seen through your ratty old disguises. An' it looks like it's checkmate for you!'

Chapter 13
And Everyone Says 'Hooray!'

'So you see,' Polly told the crowd outside the butcher's shop later that morning, 'it was Mr Gum an' Billy all along. Every night they done dressed up in their stinky old fur coat an' terrorised the town.'

'But I saw them playing chess the night the

Hound attacked me and Burger Boy,' frowned Jonathan Ripples. 'How could they be in two places at once?'

'I wondered 'bout that myself, Mr Ripples, sir,' said Polly. 'My suspicions was first 'roused when I saw Billy William a-lyin' on the butcher's shop floor. He didn't look quite right an' he wasn't movin' one tiny bit. An' then Friday's brilliant song done gave me the important clue what I needed to work it out.'

♪ *I am no baby with a dummy* ♪

sang Friday, slipping into his tap-dancing shoes
once more.

'An' it was that word – "dummy" – what done
it,' said Polly, leading the amazed crowd into the
butcher's shop where Mr Gum and Billy still sat
hunched over their chessboard.

'Splib!' trembled Old Granny. 'Watch out, Polly!'

'Don't worry,' said Polly, tugging at Mr Gum's

beard only to have it come off in her hand. 'See? They isn't nothin' but plastic shop dummies. Dummies. Jus' like Friday said in his song. The real culprits are tied up 'gainst the Oak Tree of Shame in the town square.'

'The villains also used this to aid in their ingenious illusion,' continued Friday, reaching below the counter and producing a battered old tape recorder covered in grease. 'Observe,' he said, pressing PLAY.

'Right, I got a brilliant move,' growled Mr Gum's voice from the machine. 'I'm gonna move me Bishop over there –'

But Friday had pressed STOP. He could stand to hear the villains' voices no more, and also he just enjoyed pressing buttons.

'So it was just Mr Gum and Billy up to their

usual mischief,' said David Casserole, the town mayor. 'What a terrible scheme, trying to get rid of Jake the dog like that! But you caught them, Friday. You truly are the greatest detective of them all.'

'Thank you, your majesty,' said Friday graciously, 'but I can't accept your speech. It makes me puke deep down inside where the truth really lies. The fact is, there is one greater even than I.'

And with that, he took out an imaginary

detective's razor and shaved off his imaginary detective's moustache.

'Here,' said Friday, handing the moustache to Polly. 'This belongs to you now. Put it on, little miss,' he urged, 'put it on.'

And so, with tears in her eyes, Polly donned that legendary invisible facial hair and proudly she stood there twirling it thoughtfully between her thumb and her forefinger for all to not see.

'The passing of an imaginary detective's

moustache from one generation to another is a very important occasion,' Friday told the assembled townsfolk. 'And now, would everyone please take out their 𝕷𝖎𝖙𝖙𝖑𝖊 𝕭𝖔𝖔𝖐 𝖔𝖋 𝕯𝖊𝖙𝖊𝖈𝖙𝖎𝖛𝖊 𝕳𝖞𝖒𝖓𝖘. You should each have a copy – you see, I secretly broke into all of your houses last night and placed them in your pockets while you were asleep.'

So the townsfolk reached into their pockets and just as Friday had promised, there they found copies of the **Little Book of Detective Hymns**, a handsome red volume with a picture of a falcon on the front.

'Falcons are the favourite birds of us detectives,' explained Friday. 'We admire them for six reasons, none of which any of you could possibly understand. Now – please turn to page 38. Hymn number 12 – *The Moustache Has Been Passed On.*'

And taking out his pipe organ, Friday led the townsfolk –

The moustache has been passed on!
The moustache has been passed on!
To Friday it did once belong
But now that time is past and gone
And so we sing our joyful song
The moustache has been passed on!

The moustache has been passed on!
The moustache has been passed on!
It's twirly and curly and rather long
And it once nearly got eaten by a swan
Called John the Swan who lived in Hong Kong
The moustache has been passed on!

The moustache has been passed on!
The moustache has been passed on!
There's not many words that rhyme with 'on'
We've already used 'swan' and 'John' and 'Hong Kong'
So let us end this dreadful song
The moustache has been passed on!

'What a nice gesture, Frides,' said Polly. 'An' wearin' this magnificent moustacher means I done it – I finally become a proper detective.'

And then she said, 'I've solved the crime!'

And everyone said 'hooray!'

Yes, everyone said 'hooray!'

Chapter 14
Another Case Closed

'Townsfolk,' said Polly, when the cheering had finally quietened down. 'It's all very well to do them celebratin's an' cheerin's an' such-like, but you got some massive apologisin' to do. You oughtn'ts to go whippin' up hatreds towards big friendly dogs without no proofs,' she continued, her imaginary moustache fluttering grandly in the breeze, 'an' that's a Official Polly Bit of Advice.'

'Well said, Polly,' agreed Mayor Casserole. 'We shall engrave your ancient words upon the side of the Town Hall this very day. And Martin Launderette shall be Officially Sat On by Jonathan Ripples until sundown. Now, as for the villains,' he continued, 'they are the ones that must be sent to Australia, to work on the spider farms along with all the other prisoners.'

But when he went to untie the villains from the Oak Tree of Shame, he got a nasty surprise.

Billy William's arm came away in his hand and Mr Gum's head rolled off into a flowerbed and ran over a dormouse.

'Oh, MARZIPAN,' sighed Polly. 'It's jus' them shop dummies again. The real villains must've done a crafty swap an' run off down the road, drinkin' beer an' laughin' like rattlesnakes.'

And it was true. That was exactly what had happened, and who knew when next they would return? But as everyone agreed, the important thing was that Jake the dog had been proven innocent and for the rest of that day he was treated like a king and paraded round town in a big golden taxi, barking victoriously for all to hear.

◫ ◫ ◫

But what of the little town of Lamonic Bibber itself? Well, you've never seen such a feast! Even the tramps in the duck pond were allowed a nibble. There was food and laughter and singing and dancing, and then more food and more laughter and more singing and more dancing. And then MORE food and MORE laughter and MORE singing and MORE dancing. And then everyone was sick.

And later still, when the feasting was at an end and all the vomit had been cleared up by trained badgers, Polly and Friday sat together in the town square, gazing up at a clear evening sky in which not a trace of fog could be seen. The moon was out and the twinkling stars danced a waltz in its silvery light.

'Frides,' said Polly at length. 'Whatever anyone says, you'll always be the greatest detectiver in my little eyes. I'm well proud to know you.'

'As well you should be,' said a voice from behind her. And without turning around, Polly knew it was the Spirit of the Rainbow, for she could feel the warmth of his honesty radiating from him like a miniature boy-shaped sun.

'Child,' said the Spirit of the Rainbow to Polly, even though he was no older than she. 'Because of you, the world is once more glowing with happy colours. You have done well, and you shall forever be remembered, not just in your lifetime but for many –'

'Spirit!' called a voice from the other side of the town square. 'It's yer uncle Ken on the phone! Come and talk to him!'

'Oops, gotta go,' said the Spirit of the Rainbow. And he tossed the detectives a couple of fruit chews and off he ran.

'Frides, what do you think the Spirit done meant 'bout bein' remembered forever an' ever?' asked Polly as they watched him go.

'Why, don't you know, little miss?' laughed

Friday. 'It means your words and actions are so magnificent that no one will ever forget them. Look,' he said, pointing across the square.

For the engravers had finished their work. And there upon the side of the Town Hall, just as Mayor Casserole had commanded, were Polly's words, in letters five feet high:

YOU OUGHTN'TS TO GO WHIPPIN' UP HATREDS TOWARDS BIG FRIENDLY DOGS WITHOUT NO PROOFS!

And as far as I, or anyone else knows, those words are written there still.

THE END

Outroduction

'. . . And as far as I, or anyone else knows, those words are written there still,' finished Friday, looking at his listeners in satisfaction. Alan Taylor had an expression of amazement on his face and so did Polly, although she knew the story already, so she was mostly looking amazed just to be polite.

'That was extraordinary,' said Alan Taylor admiringly. 'But I see by my chocolate wristwatch that the hour has grown late. I'd better head back home.'

'Me too,' said Polly, putting on her duffle-coat. 'Night, Frides. Thanks for the story.'

'Yes, thank you, Friday,' said Alan Taylor. 'It was a most remarkable tale.'

'I didn't really like it,' said the tulip from its vase on the mantelpiece. 'I thought it was a bit rubbish.'

'I'm sorry it wasn't to your taste,' said Friday. 'That's the trouble with these rare talking flowers,' he whispered to his guests. 'They are nice to look at but very hard to please.

'Now, goodnight and Godspeed,' he said, ushering Polly and Alan Taylor out of the front door and into the cold winter's night.

'Night, Frides!'

'Goodnight, Friday!'

Friday watched as they boarded a hansom cab, which is one of those horse-drawn carriages driven by a guy in a cloak who pulls the reins and says things like, 'Where you goin' to, guv'nor?' and 'Oh, no, there's a highwayman up ahead!' and 'To be honest, I don't really know what I'm doin' here, I actually belong in the nineteenth century.'

'What fine friends I have,' thought

Friday as Polly and Alan Taylor disappeared in a cloud of snow and horse sweat. 'But still – I can't wait until Mrs Lovely gets back.'

Mrs Lovely was Friday's wife. She was off in the Himalayas, gathering rare herbs to make her sweets and fighting off the yaks.

'I hope you come home soon, Mrs Lovely,' sighed Friday, shutting one eye so that he could gaze at the tiny photo of her which he always kept behind his left eyelid. 'I miss your kindly head and your kindly body and that thing that connects them both, what's it called again? Oh, yes – your neck.'

For a moment Friday felt a twinge of loneliness. And then – BONG! BONG! BONG! – the Bells of Charlie Nest rang out from the study, clear and bright and true. Somewhere, perhaps many thousands of miles away, someone had just bought a bread roll.

'Maybe it was even Mrs Lovely herself,' smiled Friday. 'She likes bread.'

And he closed the door on the cold and the dark, and went inside where it was warm.

FIN

THE PLUM RUFFIAN:

A USER'S GUIDE

'It had been a fine dinner, a fine dinner indeed. Roast beef with potatoes and horseradish sauce, followed by the biggest, most delicious Plum Ruffian you've ever laid eyes on . . .'

Yes, just look at those famous words. They are from a mighty book called *My Gym in 'The Hound of Lamonic Bibber'*. Have you ever heard of it? Probably not, because you can't read, you're just children.

But the question remains: Just what is a Plum Ruffian?

Well, it is a type of enormous round pudding that dates back to the days of King George II. (King George II was the sequel to King George I.

He wasn't quite as good, but he had better special effects.) The pudding is made with raisins and orange peel and nuts and spices and all sorts of stuff, and that's the body. And then you get some sticks of liquorice and stick them in the sides – and they're the arms. And then for the head, you get a plum, the biggest one you can find, and you draw an unfriendly scowling face on it. And you sit the scowling plum on top of the body and put some whipped cream on

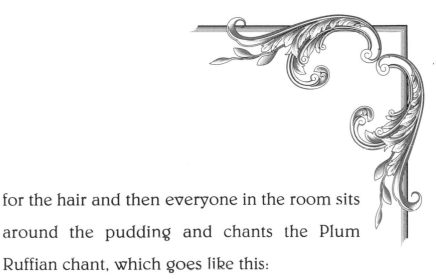

for the hair and then everyone in the room sits around the pudding and chants the Plum Ruffian chant, which goes like this:

I like plums, plums are nice!
I like plums in sugar and spice!
But what is this, what's this I see?
A naughty Plum Ruffian, staring at me!

Plum Ruffian!
Plum Ruffian!
Plum Plum Plum Plum!
Plum Ruffian!

Plum Ruffian!
Plum Ruffian!
Plum Plum Plum Plum!
Plum Ruffian!

Plum Ruffian!
Plum Ruffian!
Plum Plum Plum Plum!
Plum Ruffian!

Plum Ruffian!
Plum Ruffian!
Plum Plum Plum Plu –

Anyway. This chant goes on for about three hours. When it's over, you take some brandy and you pour it all over the pudding and then you set fire to it with a special 30-foot-long candle known as **'The Brigadoon'** and – WHOOSH! – the Plum Ruffian goes up in blue flames like the devil he is. And everyone cries,

TOODLE-LUMA-LUMA!
The Plum Ruffian has been vanquished at last!

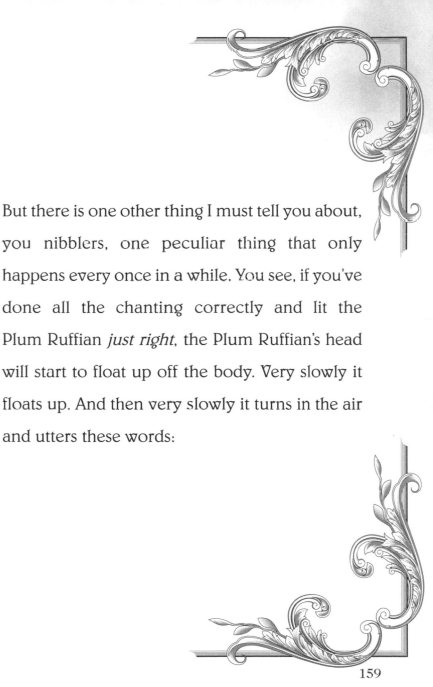

But there is one other thing I must tell you about, you nibblers, one peculiar thing that only happens every once in a while. You see, if you've done all the chanting correctly and lit the Plum Ruffian *just right*, the Plum Ruffian's head will start to float up off the body. Very slowly it floats up. And then very slowly it turns in the air and utters these words:

POOBLE-ME-NOOBLE!
YOU NEVER CATCH ME!
POOBLE-ME-NOOBLE!
ONE-TWO-THREE!

And then, very slowly, the head floats up the chimney, like a beautiful dream. And then, very slowly, it goes floating out into the night sky. And this is called 'The Plum Ruffian's Final Journey'. It is a wonderful, breathtaking moment, but if it

doesn't happen, don't worry. It has only occurred six times in the whole of history. And either way you still get to eat the rest of the pudding. And besides, if the Plum Ruffian's head *has* escaped, it is usually found the next morning, withered into a horrible prune. Bad luck, Plum Ruffian! You'll never win, you rotter!

And now you can make your very own Plum Ruffian and (with the help of a responsible adult or blackbird) defeat him with the brandy for

yourself, because here's the recipe!

The recipe for what?

The recipe for Plum Ruffians, pay attention!

What do you think I've been going on about for the last ten pages? Honestly. If you don't pay attention to what you read, anyone could SEND ME ALL YOUR MONEY AND TOYS IMMEDIATELY put all sorts of ideas into your heads DO IT NOW.

Plum Ruffian

(Serves 6–8 people)
(Or 1 Jonathan Ripples)
(Or about 800 Alan Taylors)

Ingredients

- 85g self-raising flour
- ¾ tsp ground mixed spice, by the way 'tsp' stands for 'teaspoon', or did you know that already?
  WELL, GOOD FOR YOU, YOU LITTLE SHOW-OFFS
- 140g shredded suet
- 85g fresh white breadcrumbs
- 140g dark muscovado sugar
- 140g raisins
- 100,000,000,000,000g exaggeraisins
- 140g sultanas
- 140g currants
- 25g mixed candied peel, chopped
- finely grated zest and juice of 1 poor, small, innocent orange
- finely grated zest and juice of 1 small lemon.
  Don't feel sorry for the lemon, he deserved it

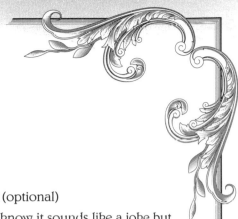

- 25g glacé cherries, chopped (optional)
- 1 small carrot, grated. Yes, I know it sounds like a joke but it's true
- 3 tbsp sweet stout. By the way, 'tbsp' stand for 'tablespoons' but I expect you knew that too, didn't you?
  YOU LITTLE SHOW-OFFS, YOU MAKE ME SICK
- 2 tsp black treacle
- brandy, to feed. I don't even know what that means, but it's in the recipe
- bottle of brandy
- 4lbs bacon
- 2 sticks of liquorice
- 1 plum, the biggest you can find
- 1 bit of whipped cream
- 1 30-foot candle (the 'Brigadoon')

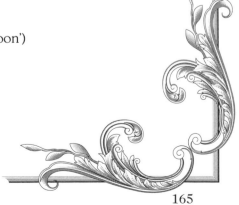

Method

1. Stir up the flour! Stir up the spice! And the suet! Just do it! And the breadcrumbs! And the sugar! Go on! Stir it all up in a big fat bowl! Tip in the fruit! And the peel! And the zest! And the (optional) cherries! And the carrot (seriously)! Then stir it all up and mix it all around! Sing while you do it, or don't make a sound! Yeah! Yeah! Yeah! Then add the rest of the ingredients and beat it! Just beat it! Until it's thoroughly combined! Good.

2. Get a spoon! Spoon the mixture into a buttered 1.2-litre pudding bowl! Put a buttered disc of greaseproof paper in the bottom first though, or you'll be in for some sticky trouble! Press the paper down well! Cover the whole dirty mess with a circle of buttered greaseproof paper! Then cover that with pudding cloth or foil! Then tie it all up securely with string, like a bad prisoner! Isn't cooking weird?

3. Stand the bowl on an upturned saucer in a saucepan! Get a responsible adult or a blackbird! NOW! Do it! Or you can't carry on! Half-fill the pan with boiling water! Cover tightly and steam it for an astounding 8 HOURS, topping up the water as necessary! Be sure to stand guard throughout that time in case any greedy clowns try to break in and run off with it! Then leave it to cool down in the pan! YEAH!

4. Remove the pudding from the pan using your own ingenuity! Discard the cloth or foil and the paper! Then cover it with some fresh greaseproof paper and cloth! What a bother it all is! Now you have to store it in a cool, dry place until required – you can feed it with a few tablespoons of brandy once in a while if you like! Oh, so that's what 'feeding' it means – just pouring brandy all over it for a laugh! Before serving, steam it again for 2 – 3 hours. It takes FOREVER!

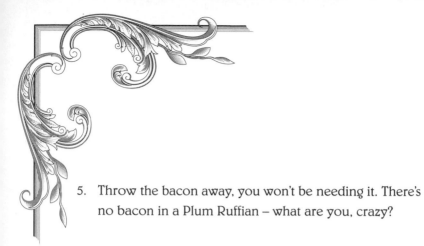

5. Throw the bacon away, you won't be needing it. There's no bacon in a Plum Ruffian – what are you, crazy?

6. NOW YOU'RE NEARLY THERE! Put the liquorice sticks in the sides to make the arms! Draw a scowling face on the plum and push it down on to the pudding to make the head! Put the whipped cream on top for the hair! Now, get chanting and have the brandy and the Brigadoon at the ready! Plum Ruffian! Plum Ruffian! Plum plum plum plum! Plum Ruffian!

GOOD LUCK, YOU GUZZLERS!

POOBLE-ME-NOOBLE!
YOU NEVER CATCH ME!

EXTRA! EXTRA! READ ALL ABOUT IT!

The Lam

'Jake the dog

» 'I'll kick him out if it's the first thing I do!' vows Martin Launderette

» 'Then I'll kick him out again, just to make sure,' he adds

Manzilla Uprooster reports

For centuries, Lamonic Bibber has been famous for three things: having a stupid name, being haunted by the ghost of William Shakespeare, and being the only place in England where it is still legal to marry a bee. But now there is a fourth reason to remember our picturesque little town: the so-called Hound of Lamonic Bibber. For the past few nights, this mysterious howling beast has run riot, ruining gardens, smashing windows, even murdering an innocent double cheeseburger, leaving only the pickled gherkins lying alone in a horrifying pool of red ketchup. But at last, one man thinks he has discovered the identity of the dirty night-time invader. 'It's Jake the dog, I'm sure of it,' local businessman Martin Launderette told our reporters. 'For a start, Jake the dog is a dog and "dog" is just another word for "hound". Secondly, Jake the dog

liv
Bib
you
Bib
ther
dog
– an
Aust
town

Rare talking flower

» 'I'm very proud,' comments owner

nical Chronicle

must go!' say townsfolk

tin Launderette: 'Jake's the one to blame!'

said Old Granny. 'Jake the dog must go!' 'Jake used to be a nice dog but now it's time to kick him out,' remarked a young girl by the name of Peter. Even Fibbles the grocer, one of Jake the dog's biggest fans, agreed that enough was enough. 'Jake once saved me from drowning,' said Mr Fibbles. 'He dragged me out of the river, brought me back to life with mouth-to-mouth resuscitation, dialled 999, barked Morse code down the line to tell them where to find me, rode with me to the hospital in the ambulance and stayed at my bedside for three weeks until I was fully recovered. And he still visits me from time to time to check that I'm OK. He's also saved the life of my sister, my aunt and five of my grandchildren. But now that I've heard Martin Launderette speaking for about three seconds, I've decided that Jake the dog is an appalling menace and we must kick him out immediately.' And Mr Fibbles' wife, Nancy, agreed. 'BZZZ,' she said, before flying off to the park to gather pollen.

onic Bibber, and the Hound of Lamonic lives in Lamonic Bibber. And thirdly, if the letters of "the Hound of Lamonic mix them all up and take out a few of d in a few others, it spells out "Jake the ne to blame". I know he's the culprit t rest easy until he's been sent off to nd it seems that there are many in ee. 'Martin Launderette's got it right,'

Jake the dog: 'Woof. Woof. Bark.'

covered in man's study

*H*ello again, crime-solving fans.

Have you ever wondered what goes on inside the mind of a famous detective? Of course you have, you're only human. Well, we can't actually climb inside a detective's mind, that would be illegal. But what we *can* do is take a look inside the actual notebook of Friday O'Leary, the greatest detective of them all . . .

The Astounding Notebook of Friday O'Leary

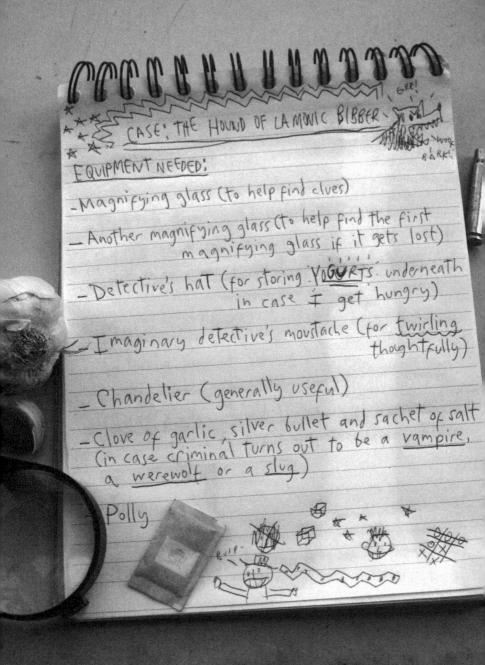

CASE: THE HOUND OF LA MOOIC BIBBER

GRR!
WOOF
BARK!

EQUIPMENT NEEDED:

- Magnifying glass (to help find clues)

- Another magnifying glass (to help find the first magnifying glass if it gets lost)

- Detective's hat (for storing YOGURTS underneath in case I get hungry)

- Imaginary detective's moustache (for twirling thoughtfully)

- Chandelier (generally useful)

- Clove of garlic, silver bullet and sachet of salt (in case criminal turns out to be a vampire, a werewolf or a slug)

- Polly

FRIDAY
4
MRS.
LOVELY

CLUES FOUND SO FAR:

? ? ? ? ? ? ? ?
? ? ? ? ? ? ? ?

- Pebble that looks a bit suspicious

- Pebble that doesn't look suspicious. But that just makes me suspect it <u>EVEN MORE.</u>

- Mysterious handkerchief. Found lying on high street with 'F O'L' written on it. Who does it belong to? ← <u>FIND OUT.</u>

- Chess piece. Found lying near scene of Hound attack. Probably not important

? ?
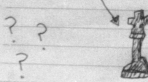
?

- Belgium. Found lying between Germany and France

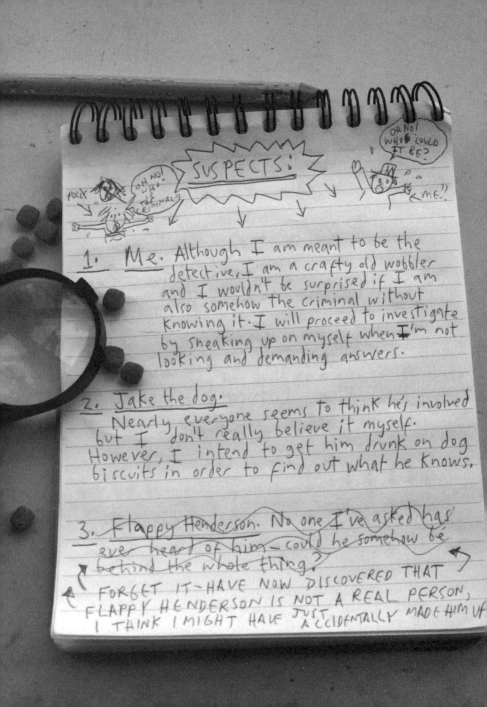

SUSPECTS:

1. **Me.** Although I am meant to be the detective, I am a crafty old wobbler and I wouldn't be surprised if I am also somehow the criminal without knowing it. I will proceed to investigate by sneaking up on myself when I'm not looking and demanding answers.

2. **Jake the dog.** Nearly everyone seems to think he's involved but I don't really believe it myself. However, I intend to get him drunk on dog biscuits in order to find out what he knows.

3. **Flappy Henderson.** No one I've asked has ever heard of him — could he somehow be behind the whole thing?

FORGET IT — HAVE NOW DISCOVERED THAT FLAPPY HENDERSON IS NOT A REAL PERSON, I THINK I MIGHT HAVE JUST ACCIDENTALLY MADE HIM UP

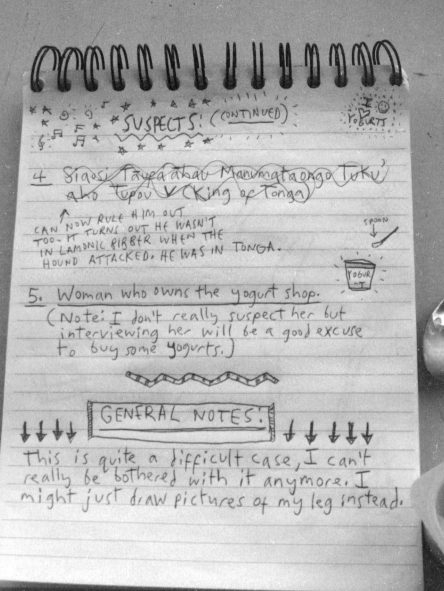

SUSPECTS: (CONTINUED)

4. Siaosi Tāvea ahav Manumataongo Tuku' aho Tupou V (King of Tonga)

↑ CAN NOW RULE HIM OUT
TOO - IT TURNS OUT HE WASN'T
IN LAMONIC RIBBER WHEN THE
HOUND ATTACKED. HE WAS IN TONGA.

SPOON →

YOGUR T

5. Woman who owns the yogurt shop.
(Note: I don't really suspect her but interviewing her will be a good excuse to buy some yogurts.)

GENERAL NOTES:

↓↓↓↓   ↓↓↓↓↓

This is quite a difficult case, I can't really be bothered with it anymore. I might just draw pictures of my leg instead.

RICK!

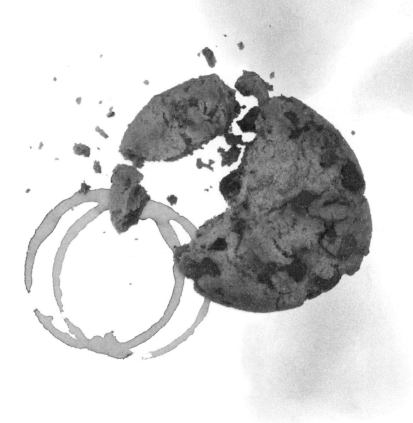

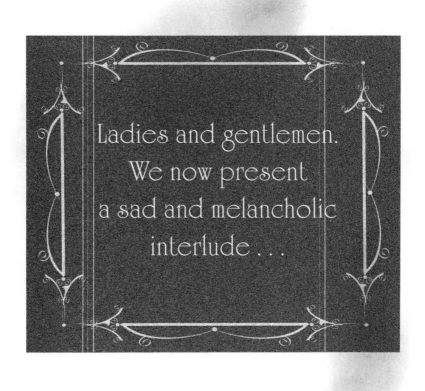

Ladies and gentlemen.
We now present
a sad and melancholic
interlude . . .

The Love Song of J. Alfred Ripples

It was raining in Lamonic Bibber, a thin grey drizzle that got down the back of your jumper and made your neck itch – but Jonathan Ripples cared not, for nothing could compare to the endless rain that fell in his fat, lonely heart.

'Why?' he said, as he stood beneath a stone statue of an oak tree in the town square. 'Why were you taken from me so cruelly, Burger Boy? Why?'

But no answer came from the wind or the rain, no answer came from the cold wet earth, no answer came from the glowering sky. A soggy old pigeon with half its feathers missing went 'CAAWWWK', but that wasn't really an answer either, it probably would have done that anyway.

'Burger Boy,' said Jonathan Ripples at length. 'I know you can never return. But I have written a poem in your memory.'

And clearing his throat, he began:

ODE TO A DOUBLE CHEESEBURGER
By Jonathan Alfred Ripples (me)

Oh, Burger Boy, Burger Boy, Burger Boy
Thou were the most beautiful thing I ever did see
With thy bun as smooth as an angel's kiss
Thy cheese as yellow as the Evening star
Thy sauce as red as an Arabian ruby
Thy tomatoes not quite as red as thy sauce
but still quite red
And who could forget thy gherkins,
solemn and wise?
Oh, Burger Boy, Burger Boy, Burger Boy, oh!
Where thou art now, nobody doth know.

Oh, Burger Boy, Burger Boy, Burger Boy
For many long hours did I look forward
to eating you gently
Savouring every delightful flavour you did possess
But – alas! Thou were snatched
by the cruel paws of Fate!
By men of ill-favour disguised as a beast!
Thou, who were so noble, gentle and kind
Were savagely scoffed by those scoundrels unpleasant
Thy bun left half-eaten and covered in spit
At the side of the road, to be pecked at by crows
Oh, Burger Boy, Burger Boy, Burger Boy, oh!
Where thou art now, nobody doth know.

Oh, Burger Boy, Burger Boy, Burger Boy
'Tis time for me to leave and get some lunch now
Perchance I might get a Cornish pasty from that
place that does those nice homemade ones,
dost thou know where I mean?
'Tis that place next to the newsagent's
on the high street
It only opened recently and 'tis very
reasonably priced
and you can get a special 'Meal Deal'
with crisps and a fizzy drink for
only a pound more.

Or perhaps I will heat up
last night's chilli con carne in the microwave.
But, oh, my beefy darling! Think not for a moment
That I shall ever love another meal
as much as I did love you.
For tho' thou never did make it to my belly
Thou hast forever found a place
deep inside my heart.
Oh, Burger Boy, Burger Boy, Burger Boy, ee!
Wherever thou art now, think kindly of me.

The last of the beautiful words faded away on the wind. For a moment longer, Jonathan Ripples lingered beneath the statue of the oak tree, thinking about life and death and everything in between. And then, very slowly, he walked out of the town square and towards his next square meal.

Well, that was miserable, wasn't it? Sorry about that.

AND NOW... QUESTIONS! QUESTIONS! QUESTIONS! FLOODING INTO THE MINDS OF CONCERNED YOUNG CHILDREN TODAY...

Why do objects move around all the time, I mean, even if you're just in a small room and you're using a pencil and you put it down for about one second and then try to find it again, it's gone! I mean, how on earth does that happe– oh, there it is, it rolled off the desk on to the floor. But still, it's so weird. Objects aren't supposed to move and yet they move around ALL THE TIME! Why?

A Well, the answer to this one is simple. I have it here, written on a piece of pape–hold on, where's that piece of paper got to? Honestly, I had it just a minute ago. Sorry. Next question!

Q If you get fake wings and strap them to everyone's backs and then tie everyone to invisible wires so it looks like they're flying, and then act like it's completely normal in front of a baby who's never seen people before, will that baby grow real wings and learn to fly?

A Yes, babies' brains are trained to copy everything they see. After about a week of looking at everyone else hovering around, the baby's brain will think that's how things should be done and send a signal to the body telling it to hurry up and make some enormous wings. Within a week the wings will have sprouted and within a month the baby will be flying around without a care in the world. That is also how birds were invented – by tricking a baby vole.

193

Q How did Mr Gum and Billy William the Third become friends?

194

A Well, that is a very good question, far better than your other ones, which I thought were quite ridiculous, to be honest.

Mr Gum and Billy met way back in the old days when they were just young lads. Here, take a look for yourself . . .

Young Master Gum Makes a Friend

Young Master Gum was a ten-year-old boy with a red beard and two bloodshot eyes that stared out at you like a ten-year-old octopus curled up in a bad cave. He was a complete horror who hated children (even though he was one), animals and fun. What he liked was scribbling all over library books, sitting in his filthy living room, and saying 'I wonder what's on TV'.

'I wonder what's on TV,' said Master Gum one afternoon as he sat in his filthy living room, scribbling all over library books. 'Shabba me young boy's whiskers! They're showin' The Queen Eating Wafers again.'

It was true. Back in those days, there were only three TV channels in the whole of England: BBC1, BBC2 and Upside-Down BBC2, which was just the same as BBC2, only you stood on your head to pretend it was a different channel. And the only programme that was ever on was The Queen Eating Wafers.

'Stupid Queen!' growled Master Gum. 'Stupid wafers! I wish they'd hurry up an' invent a programme about somethin' useful, like some sticks in a bag or somethin'. But that'll never happen. Stupid everythin'!'

'Mmm,' said the Queen as she ate another

wafer on TV. 'It's brilliant being the Queen. Free wafers all day, plus I'm on TV all the time. What a laugh it all is! I'm glad I'm the Queen instead of you, Master Gum! Ha ha ha!'

'Shabba me whiskers!' growled Master Gum, switching the TV off by kicking it in with his boot, smashing it up with a sledgehammer, throwing it out the lounge window, running outside, hopping up and down all over the bits, sweeping the bits up into a cardboard box, running down the road with the cardboard box on his shoulder, hopping on a bus for forty-five minutes, hopping off the bus, throwing the cardboard box over a cliff into the sea and running back home again.

'What a borin' flippin' life I lead,' he said once he was back home. 'I wonder what's on TV.'

Master Gum went to turn on his TV but of course it wasn't there anymore. It was nothing but dust, floating around the ocean and poisoning wildlife.

'Oh, yeah,' he said. 'I forgot I kicked the TV in. What a bother.'

Master Gum sat back in his broken armchair and amused himself by spitting up into the air and waiting to see if the spit landed on his face. It always did.

'I'm the best at this!' he laughed. But eventually he ran out of spit.

'I better go an' get some more,' he scowled. So off he stomped, out of the house and down the street, to get some more spit from the spit shop.

Now, in those old-fashioned days, there were only four shops in the whole of Lamonic Bibber. There was a shop that sold wheat, another shop that sold half-price wheat and another shop that gave the wheat away for free. It was a very competitive business. And then there was Billy William the Second's Palace of Spit, run by a miserable old geezer called Billy William the Second.

Master Gum was secretly a bit scared of Old Man Billy – in fact, all the children of the town were, and all sorts of legends had grown up around him. Some of the children said that if you whispered, *'Old Man Billy, where are my eyes?'* three times at midnight, then Old Man Billy would appear at your window with stolen diamonds in his mouth. Some of them said that Old Man Billy had once been a famous murderer in a far-off country called Madeupia. And some of them said that Old Man Billy could crawl through any space, no matter how small.

Young Master Gum didn't believe all the stories he had heard but he was still careful to be polite whenever he went into the spit shop, because Old Man Billy had a nasty habit of bashing you with his fists when you weren't looking. And when you *were* looking, he'd bash you again, twice as hard as before.

'That'll teach you for lookin',' Old Man Billy would grumble. And then he'd laugh so hard his wooden leg would fall off, even though he didn't have a wooden leg.

'Good mornin', Old Man Billy,' said Master Gum now, as he walked into Billy William the Second's Palace of Spit.

'I don't see what's so "good" about it,' sneered Old Man Billy.

'All right,' said Master Gum. 'Mornin', Old Man Billy.'

'I don't see what's so "morning" about it,' sneered Old Man Billy, pointing to his wristwatch.

'Look, it's the afternoon, you ignorant swiper.'

'Oh, yeah,' said Master Gum. 'Well, never mind that now, you strange old bloke what scares me quite a lot. I wanna buy some spit. I used up all mine gobbin' it on me own face cos I'm so brilliant.'

'No chance of that, beardboy,' said Old Man Billy. 'I'm all out of spit. I sold me last bucket to the Queen ten minutes ago. Her mouth gets terrible dry cos of all them wafers she's always eatin', so she took the lot.'

'Shabba me whiskers!' growled Master Gum. 'Stupid blibberin' monarch!'

'OI!' yelled Old Man Billy, clipping Master Gum around the ear. 'No swearin' in my shop, you filthy-mouthed crumb! I'm in a bad enough mood already.'

'Oh, yeah?' said Master Gum. 'An' why's that then?'

'I'll tell you why,' said Old Man Billy. 'Jus' this mornin' I come downstairs an' I noticed *this* little swiper.'

Old Man Billy pointed to a scrawny boy in a butcher's cap and apron who was cowering in the corner, dribble coming out of his nose. Master Gum hadn't noticed him there before because the shop was so dark and dingy, and also – well, that was really the reason, it was just because the shop was so dark and dingy, there wasn't any other reason he hadn't noticed him, that was it. Anyway, he hadn't noticed him there before.

'He says he's my son,' said Old Man Billy. 'He says his name's Billy William the Third. He says he's been standin' in that corner ever since he was a baby.'

'What, didn't you notice him there before?' said Master Gum in astonishment.

'Nah,' said Old Man

Billy. 'This shop's so dark an' dingy, I never saw him there. I never even knew I had a son.'

'Why's he dressed as a butcher?' said Master Gum.

'I dunno,' said Old Man Billy, punching Master Gum's hat so hard that his fist went through and came out the other side. 'Who cares? Anyway, I don't want no son. You can have him if you want.'

'OK,' said Master Gum. 'Thanks.'

And so Master Gum left the shop with Billy

William the Third following along behind him like a disgraced bean.

'What you squintin' at?' scowled Master Gum as he and Billy William the Third walked down the road together.

'It's the sunlight, Master Gum, me old new best friend,' replied Billy. 'I never seen it before cos I never been outside. In fact, I didn't even know it was called "sunlight", that was just a lucky guess.'

'Well, stick with me an' I'll teach you

everythin',' grinned Master Gum, who saw he could have some fun with Billy. 'See that thing over there?' he said, pointing to a screwdriver lying on the pavement.

'Yeah?' said Billy.

'That's called a "Matthew Robinson",' said Master Gum. And from that day to this, Billy William the Third has always thought that screwdrivers are called 'Matthew Robinsons'.

As Billy and Master Gum walked along, they saw a young boy on his hands and knees in the town square, digging in the dirt.

'Who's that?' said Billy.

'That's young Master Friday O'Leary,' scowled Master Gum. 'Don't you go near him, Billy me boy. He's a weirdo an' a menace an' he's always up to somethin' or other what I simply cannot stand.'

'What's he doin'?' asked Billy.

'I'm planting a stone acorn,' answered Master

O'Leary cheerfully. 'One day it will grow into a wonderful stone statue of an oak tree. And people can sit beneath its lovely stone branches and enjoy the shade for generations to come. THE TRUTH IS FLOUR, BUTTER, EGGS, CORNFLOUR, CASTER SUGAR, FINELY GRATED LEMON ZEST AND FRESH LEMON JUICE!'

(You see, as a young boy, Master O'Leary already had all the ingredients for the truth – he just hadn't put them together yet.)

'Told you he was a weirdo,' said Master Gum.

'I reckon we oughta –'

But just then the cry went up:

'Pillows! I have got some pillows! Do you want any pillows? I have got some pillows!'

'Well, flip me kidneys into a bush an' call me a mechanical burp!' exclaimed Master Gum, forgetting all about Master O'Leary. 'It's Ned Needles!'

Now, Ned Needles was a travelling pillow salesman. Up and down the land he rode on his great shire horse, selling pillows to one and all.

His horse's name was Handsome and you could see why, for no nobler animal ever did walk the earth. Ned loved him to bits, even though Handsome had accidentally killed his entire family by treading on them.

'Pillows!' cried Ned Needles again. 'Who wants some pillows?'

'What are "pillows"?' whispered Billy William.

'Shut up,' said Master Gum, stamping on Billy's foot to teach him a lesson. The lesson was that it hurts when people stamp on your foot. 'Pillows is magnificent. Pillows is what you rest your head on when you lie down in yer bed for a crafty snooze.'

'I don't even know what a bed is,' laughed Billy. 'I used to sleep standin' up in the corner of the spit shop.'

'Well, mark my words,' said Master Gum. 'Pillows is superb. An' I fancies one! OI, NEEDLES! Give us one of them pillows!'

'G-g-good day to you, young gentlemen,' said Ned Needles, bringing his horse to a stop by pressing the 'OFF' button behind Handsome's left ear. 'W-w-what a pleasure it i-is to m-meet you both.'

'Enough of yer talkin' you nervous shrimp!' laughed Master Gum. 'I wanna see yer finest pillow an' I wanna see it NOW!'

'Yeah,' said Billy William, who was busy pulling Handsome's tail to see if it would make him lay an egg or do a fart or something.

'R-right you are, young gents,' stammered Ned Needles, jumping down from the saddle. 'Handsome, show them the g-goods.'

At his master's command, Handsome opened his great mouth – and inside, resting on his soft pink tongue, was a marvellous pure white pillow.

'It is made of the finest s-silk,' said Ned Needles. 'And s-s-stuffed with the finest goose f-feathers.'

Master Gum inspected the pillow and his bloodshot eyes lit up like stolen crackers.

'Ever so comfy,' he murmured. 'How much do you want for it?'

'6p,' said Ned Needles. You see, 6p was a lot of money in those days, much more than 5p, for example.

'That's a shame,' said Billy William. 'Cos we ain't got any money, not a penny. Oh, well. Never mind.'

'Billy me boy,' grinned Master Gum. 'You don't know nothin' 'bout how the world works. Here's how we do things 'round here!'

And with that he snatched the pillow from Ned Needles and pushed him into the dirt. Getting the idea, Billy kicked Handsome in the leg for good measure.

'Ha ha ha!' laughed Master Gum. 'You little shrimp!' he shouted at Ned Needles. 'You pathetic little boo-flake!'

And off they ran down the road, Billy and Master Gum, carrying the fine pillow above their heads like hunters returning from the chase.

'That was brilliant,' said Billy as they

approached the high street. 'It's great bein' your best friend, Master Gum. Oh, well. I s'pose I better be gettin' back to the spit shop now.'

But just then they heard a terrible cawing noise.

And looking up they were startled to see Old Man Billy being carried off by a giant crow.

'You dirty swiper!' roared Old Man Billy. 'Put me down, put me down I say!'

But the great bird paid him no heed, and the two boys watched as it disappeared into the distance.

'Well, that's the end of him,' laughed Master Gum. 'He'll be eaten, high up in that feathery devil's nest. Chomp, chomp, chomp, beak, chomp.'

'Good,' said Billy William the Third. 'He was a completely rubbish dad an' I'm glad he's gone. Now I can have the shop for meself an' I can be what I always dreamed of bein' – a lovely florist what sells beautiful roses an' makes everyone happy.'

'That's a stupid idea,' said Master Gum. 'Why don't you be a butcher instead? Seein' as you already got a butcher's apron on.'

'OK, then,' laughed Billy William the Third. Not a nice laugh like you or I would do, but a sneaky old laugh on the inside, where nobody else could see. 'A butcher I will be, Master G, a butcher I will be! With a hig an' a hog an' a jiggety-jog, a bu– OOF! Somethin' just kicked me in the head!'

'Shut up,' growled Master Gum, who had climbed up a nearby stepladder so he could do a surprise attack on Billy from above. 'Now, you're meant to be a butcher, aintcha? Well, why ain't we got any scoffs? I'm absolutely starvin' me knuckles off here!'

'Don't you worry 'bout that,' said Billy William the Third, sniffing the air with his long quivering nose. 'This way!'

The two boys walked down a dirty overgrown alleyway and there they found a battered metal dustbin, leaning drunkenly against an ants' nest in the last dying shaft of afternoon sunlight.

'It's beautiful,' sighed Master Gum.

'Let's see what treasure's inside,' said Billy, and he lifted the lid to reveal a pile of sloppy meat and entrails amidst the rubbish. 'Oho! Looks like we're in luck!'

And so the two boys sat there, chomping away contentedly as the flies buzzed all around them.

A scraggy alley cat wailed a lonesome song called 'AIN'T GOT NO FUR'. The first rats were coming out to play in the shadows.

'Well, Billy,' said Master Gum as he sucked down a chicken liver. 'I thought you was nothin' but a useless idiot – but I was wrong. You're actually quite a useful idiot. I got a feelin' you an' me is gonna go far together, specially me.'

And from that day to this, Mr Gum and Billy have been the very best of friends.

THE END

About the Author

Andy Stanton lives in North London. He studied English at Oxford but they kicked him out. He has been a film script reader, a cartoonist, an NHS lackey and lots of other things. He has many interests, but best of all he likes cartoons, books and music (even jazz). One day he'd like to live in New York or Berlin or one of those places because he's got fantasies of bohemia. His favourite expression is 'I haven't got a favourite expression' and his favourite word is 'is'.

About the Illustrator

David Tazzyman lives in South London with his girlfriend, Melanie, and their son, Stanley. He grew up in Leicester, studied illustration at Manchester Metropolitan University and then travelled around Asia for three years before moving to London in 1997. He likes football, cricket, biscuits, music and drawing. He still dislikes celery.

www.mrgum.co.uk

You've read the book, now visit the 82% official
Mr Gum website at: www.mrgum.co.uk
It's full to bursting with things like:

AN EPISODE OF THE ALBTA award-winning
'Bag of Sticks'

BUTCHER'S DARTS!

BOOK INFORMATION AND NEWS!

PHOTOS!

Ask Andy: A chance to submit your very own
question to Mr Andy Stanton!

The Lamonical Chronicle
(see over for more details)

In fact, there are so many things on the website we can't
even be bothered trying to fit them all on this page.

Read All About it!

The Lamonical Chronicle

Visit www.mrgum.co.uk to subscribe to Lamonic Bibber's second best, & only, newspaper.

It's free! And you can win prizes!

Huzzah!

HEY, JONAH!

How much fun are the audiobook thingy versions of *Mr Gum*?

HA HA HA! HA! HA! HAHAHAHHA!
CHORTLE! **SNICKER!** HA HA!
ERK! HA! **OOP!** HA HA AH AHA!
HA! HA! HA HA HA!

EEP! **NORP!**

HA HA
HA HA
EEEP!

SNORTLE!

Yes, Jonah is exactly 100% correct. The 'Mr Gum' audiobook thingies are so funny you won't be able to speak, maybe forever. And guess who reads them out? Me! And guess who I am? Andy Stanton! So get them today, you nibbleheads, and experience the fun – it's like reading a book with your ears!

Available on CD, over the internet, by phone or inside the bellies of magic frogs. To order a copy or for more information go to www.bbcshop.com or phone 01225 443400.

(Headphones not supplied. But maybe you can borrow a spare pair off Jonah, he seems to have far too many.)